Race Further with Reading

Betty Q Investigates

By Karyn Gorman

Illustrated by Maddy McClellan

Crabtree Publishing Company

www.crabtreebooks.com

Crabtree Publishing Company
www.crabtreebooks.com
1-800-387-7650

616 Welland Ave.   PMB 59051, 350 Fifth Ave.
St. Catharines, ON   59th Floor,
L2M 5V6   New York, NY 10118

Published by Crabtree Publishing Company in 2016

First published in 2014 by Franklin Watts
(A division of Hachette Children's Books)

Text © Karyn Gorman 2014
Illustration © Maddy McClellan 2014

Series editor: Melanie Palmer
Series advisor: Catherine Glavina
Series designer: Cathryn Gilbert
Editor: Kathy Middleton
**Proofreader and
  notes to adults:** Shannon Welbourn
**Production coordinator and
  Prepress technician:** Ken Wright
Print coordinator: Amy Salter

Printed in the USA/082015/SN20150529

**Library and Archives Canada
Cataloguing in Publication**

Gorman, Karyn, author
        Betty Q investigates / Karyn Gorman ;
Maddy McClellan, illustrator.

(Race further with reading)
Issued in print and electronic formats.
ISBN 978-0-7787-2029-4 (bound).--
ISBN 978-0-7787-2090-4 (pbk.).--
ISBN 978-1-4271-1664-2 (pdf).--
ISBN 978-1-4271-1656-7 (html)

        I. McCellan, Maddy, illustrator II. Title.

PZ7.G66Be 2015   j823'.92   C2015-903050-1
                                      C2015-903051-X

**Library of Congress
Cataloging-in-Publication Data**

CIP available at Library of Congress

CHAPTER 1
Not Just a Regular Kid

From the beginning, Mr. and Mrs. Q knew their baby daughter was smart. After all, it's not every day you see a baby looking after the family's finances.

But Betty Q was more than smart. She was like a walking computer in ballet slippers.

"Betty, what's a six letter word meaning one and only?" asked Dad.

"Unique," chirped Betty.

"Your new invention works like a charm," Mom said.

"Just something I've been playing around with," said Betty.

Of course, once word got out, things got

pretty busy around the Q residence.

Everyone wanted Betty Q's help,

and the doorbell didn't

stop ringing!

Ding Dong!

"We're here to recruit Betty Q,"

said a government official.

Ding Dong!

"Ever considered the space

program, Betty Q?"

Ding Dong!

"Who is it, Betty?" asked Mom.

"No one important,"

answered Betty.

Nevertheless, Betty Q turned them all down.

She just wanted to be a regular kid

and do regular kid things.

But in Betty's hometown of Dullville,

regular things never seemed to happen.

CHAPTER 2
The Cupcake Conundrum

At school one Friday morning,
Miss Marshall discovered that Molly's
birthday cupcakes were missing. Cupcakes
were always a big hit in the classroom,
but when Miss Marshall opened the box,
all that was left were the crumbs!

Immediately, the children started to blame each other.

"It was Reggie," accused Jenny.

"He always wants more food."

"It was Jenny," shouted Reggie.

"She likes anything that's pink."

Miss Marshall explained that Molly's dad had dropped off the cupcakes the night before. The cupcakes went missing before anyone had arrived at school.

"They must have been stolen last night," said Reggie. "The school was burgled!"

Soon Principal Pio arrived to see what all the fuss was about. He confirmed that nothing else was missing and all the windows and doors were intact.

"The school was not burgled," he said.

"Then someone must have had a key," pointed out Shannon. "But who has a key to the school?"

11

The children considered the suspects.

"Caretakers have keys," said Jenny.

Caretaker Smith suddenly looked very uncomfortable.

"It wasn't me! I wasn't even here last night," protested Caretaker Smith.

"Look, the garbage cans are still full."

"A likely story," huffed Reggie.

"It's true," continued Caretaker Smith.

"I was at the big bingo tournament and

I won."

Caretaker Smith's alibi was pretty good.

Everyone was puzzled.

"What a conundrum," said Principal Pio.

"Maybe Molly's dad forgot to put the cupcakes in the box," said Reggie.

"Maybe the cupcakes just disappeared," suggested Shannon.

"Maybe there's a ghost," squeaked Billy.

"I have the answer," said Betty Q.

CHAPTER 3
The Culprit Revealed

As always, Betty Q was doing two very

important things that she always did:

listening and observing. She walked

very slowly around the room, got out

her magnifying glass, and began.

"I know who stole the cupcakes, and the thief is here in this room."

Now Betty had everyone's attention.

"Let's review the facts," she continued.

"One: Miss Marshall put the cupcakes on the highest shelf, so the thief had to reach up high."

"That's true," said Miss Marshall. "I put the cupcakes on the "Very Important Things" shelf, for safekeeping."

"Two: I noticed crumbs on the floor.
The thief must have eaten the cupcakes
inside the classroom."

"So, the thief had to be able to reach up high

and have access to the classroom,"

deduced Jenny.

"Oh my goodness, children! Don't look at me!" exclaimed Principal Pio.

"It wasn't Principal Pio," said Betty Q.

"But you said the thief had to reach the top shelf," objected Jack. "Only someone who is tall could do that."

"And you said the thief ate the cupcakes inside the classroom," said Shannon. "Who else could get in without a key?"

"You don't have to get inside the classroom if you've never left it," Betty said. "And you don't have to be tall if you can...fly! And three: Probably the most important evidence of all, the thief did not finish eating the cupcakes."

"Here's your thief!"
announced Betty Q.
"Jo-Jo!" cried
the children.

"But what about the cupcakes?" sniffed

Molly. "We won't have any for my party."

"Don't worry," said Miss Marshall.

"Luckily there are still plenty of treats

Jo-Jo hasn't been able to eat."

"Mystery solved thanks to Betty Q,"
said Principal Pio, congratulating her.
But cupcakes weren't the only thing to go
missing in Dullville that day. Betty was
about to get her biggest case yet.

"Betty, come quickly!" Wendy called.

"Patty Packer's pet shop has just
been robbed!"

CHAPTER 4
The Disappearing Dog

Betty Q and her friends ran to Patty Packer's

pet shop and found her pouting on

the porch.

"It's a disaster," she wailed. "My perfect

poodle, Snowflake, has been stolen!"

Patty's prized pooch was supposed to compete in the Dullville Pet Show later that afternoon. But when Patty returned to pick up Snowflake from the shop, she was gone.

"Minny, my shop assistant, said there were only three people in the shop today," said Patty. Then she walked over to a pen full of poodles and added some biscuits to their bowl. A group of black poodles raced over. "Snowflake would have won first prize today for sure," sniffed Patty.

"Would you mind if we talked to Minny?"

Betty asked. Minny was by the shelves,

stacking tins of dog food.

"How do we know Minny didn't take

Snowflake?" asked Reggie.

"I would never hurt Snowflake," Minny

gasped. "I put Snowflake in the poodle pen

with the other dogs this morning. I fed the

dogs at noon and Snowflake was still there."

"But when I got here at two o'clock, Snowflake was missing," said Patty.

"Who else was in the shop?" asked Jenny.

"There was one customer who bought a kitten this morning," said Minny. "And in the afternoon, another customer bought a lizard. At the same time, a delivery person dropped off fresh-cut flowers."

"I bet it was the lizard customer," said
Shannon. "After all, who buys a lizard
as a pet anyway?"

Minny shook her head. "I was with him the
whole time. He did not steal Snowflake."

"Maybe someone came into the shop
without you knowing," offered Reggie.

"We keep the doors locked so that no
animals get out," said Patty. "Everyone must
be let in and out of the shop with a key."

"May we walk around?" asked Betty Q.
As always, Betty Q was doing two very
important things that she always did:
listening and observing.

"It's as if Snowflake vanished into thin air," sniffled Patty.

Betty got out her magnifying glass. "I know exactly where Snowflake is," she declared.

CHAPTER 5
Mystery Solved!

Now Betty had everyone's attention.

"Let's review the facts," she began.

"There is only one door to the shop,"

said Betty. "And that door is locked

except when Minny opens it with a key."

"Right. I only opened and closed it three times," Minny confirmed. "And no one left with Snowflake."

"After the kitten customer left this morning, Snowflake was still in her pen," stated Betty. "Correct," confirmed Minny.

"And you were with the lizard customer the whole time," Betty continued.

"Correct," confirmed Minny.

"Of course, if you were busy with the lizard customer, then you couldn't have been watching the man delivering flowers," deduced Betty.

"But he just dropped the flowers off," said Minny. "And when I let him out of the shop, he didn't have Snowflake."

Betty walked over to the flowers on the counter. "You said that the man delivered fresh-cut flowers," said Betty.

"Yes, we get them every week," said Patty.

Betty took out one of the flowers and held it up to Patty's nose.

"What do you smell?"asked Betty.

"I can't smell anything," said Patty.

"That's right," said Betty. "Because these flowers are fake."

"But why would someone deliver fake, fresh-cut flowers?" asked Reggie.

"Because someone wanted to use the vase to hold something else instead of water," said Betty. Then she emptied the vase. Out popped a bottle of black paint.

"What is the paint for?" asked Jenny.

Betty walked over to the poodle pen and picked up one of the dogs. She took it to the dog bath and ran the water over it. "To paint a white poodle black," said Betty, turning around to reveal a white poodle.

"Snowflake!" everyone yelled.

"While Minny was distracted with the customer looking for a lizard, the man delivering flowers painted the only white dog in the shop black to match the other poodles."

"Oh, thank you, Betty Q," said Patty, holding onto Snowflake tightly.

"I bet that wasn't a real delivery person. It was probably Mr. Barker. His parrot is competing in the pet show today, too."

"Well there's still time to clean up Snowflake for the competition," said Betty. "Good luck!"

"Good work, Betty. Another case solved," Billy said, as Betty and her friends walked back to school.

"And to think Mr. Barker almost got away with his evil plan. Without Snowflake competing, Mr. Barker's parrot would have won the Dullville Pet Show for sure."

"Oh, I doubt that," Betty said with a smile. "Mr. Barker's pet can sing, but it's hard for a parrot to sing with a stomachache. Or should I say cupcake-ache?"

"You mean…?" Jenny gasped.

Betty Q nodded. "Jo-Jo is Mr. Barker's pet parrot. Mr. Barker loaned him to the school for National Pet Week. But while he was busy scheming, his parrot was eating too many cupcakes!"

"It serves Mr. Barker right," giggled Molly. "Speaking of cupcakes, can we have my party now?"

"Of course," said Miss Marshall. "Hopefully the rest of our day will be nothing but... regular."

Of course, in Betty's hometown of Dullville, regular things never seem to happen...

"Betty, come quick!"

They *still* try to recruit her

for government services.

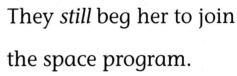

They *still* beg her to join

the space program.

And they *still* consult her on important

issues (which we still can't talk about).

But Betty Q has her hands full...

...just being a kid.

Notes for Adults

Race Further with Reading is the next entertaining level up for young readers from *Race Ahead with Reading*. Longer, more in-depth chapters and fun illustrations help children build up their vocabulary and reading skills in a fun way.

THE FOLLOWING BEFORE, DURING, AND AFTER READING ACTIVITY SUGGESTIONS SUPPORT LITERACY SKILL DEVELOPMENT AND CAN ENRICH SHARED READING EXPERIENCES:

BEFORE

1. Make reading fun! Choose a time to read when you and the reader are relaxed and have time to share the story together. Don't forget to give praise! Children learn best in a positive environment.

2. Before reading, ask the reader to look at the title and illustrations on the cover of the book **Betty Q Investigates.** Invite them to make predictions about what will happen in the story. They may make use of prior knowledge and make connections to other stories they have heard or read about a similar character.

DURING

3. Encourage readers to determine unfamiliar words themselves by using clues from the text and illustrations.

4. During reading, encourage the child to review his or her understanding and see if they want to revise their predictions midway. Encourage the reader to make text-to-text connections, choosing a part of the story that reminds them of another story they have read; and text-to-self connections, choosing a part of the story that relates to their own personal experiences; and text-to-world connections, choosing a part of the story that reminds them of something that happened in the real world.

AFTER

5. Ask the reader who the main characters are. Describe how the characters' traits or feelings impact the story.

6. Have the child retell the story in their own words. Ask him or her to think about the predictions they made before reading the story. How were they the same or different?

7. Encourage the reader to refer to parts in the story by the chapters the events occurred in and explain how the story developed.

DISCUSSION QUESTIONS FOR KIDS

8. Throughout this story, Betty Q investigates to solve various mysteries. What important things does Betty always do to work through these problems?

9. Choose one of the illustrations from the story. How do the details in the picture help you understand a part of the story better? Or, what do the illustrations tell you that is not in the text?

10. What part of the story surprised you? Why was it a surprise?

11. From your point of view, and before Betty Q solved the cases, what did you think happened to the cupcakes from Miss Marshall's classroom and Snowflake from Patty Packer's pet shop?

12. What moral, or lesson, can you take from this story?

13. Create your own story or drawing about something you had to investigate or a mystery that you solved.

14. Have you read another story by the same author? Compare the stories you have read by the same author or compare this story to other books in the *Race Further with Reading* series.

15. What is your favorite thing about being a kid? Explain.